The Dragonsitter Takes Off

First published in 2013 by
, Andersen Press Limited
20 Vauxhall Bridge Road
London SW1V 2SA
www.andersenpress.co.uk

2 4 6 8 10 9 7 5 3 1

British Library Cataloguing in Publication Data available.

ISBN 978 1 849 39571 7

Printed and bound in Great Britain by
CPI Group (UK) Ltd, Croydon, CR0 4YY

The Dragonsitter Takes Off

Josh Lacey

Illustrated by Garry Parsons

Andersen Press
London

Dear Uncle Morton,

I know you don't want to be disturbed, but I have to tell you some very bad news.

Ziggy has disappeared.

Mum says he was asleep on the carpet when she went to bed, but this morning he was nowhere to be seen.

I'm really sorry, Uncle Morton. We've only been looking after him for one night, and he's run away already.

He must hate being here.

Actually he did seem depressed when you dropped him off. I bought him a box of Maltesers as a present, but he didn't eat a single one.

I've been reading your notes. There's lots of useful information about meal times and clipping his claws, but nothing about what to do if he disappears.

Should we be searching for him, Uncle Morton? If so, where?

Eddie

Dear Uncle Morton,

We're back from school and Ziggy still isn't here.

While we were walking home, Emily said she saw him having beans on toast in the café.

I was already running to fetch him when she yelled, "Just joking!"

I don't know why she thinks she's funny, because she's really not.

Mum rang Mr McDougall. He said he would row to your island first thing tomorrow morning and look for Ziggy. He can't go now because there's a storm.

I'll let you know as soon as we hear from him.

Eddie

Dear Uncle Morton,

Don't worry about my other two emails. We have found Ziggy.

He was in the linen cupboard. I suppose he'd crawled in there because it's nice and warm.

Mum was actually the one who found him. You would have thought she'd be pleased, but in fact she was furious. She said she didn't want a dirty dragon messing up her clean sheets. She grabbed him by the nose and tried to pull him out. He didn't like that at all. Luckily Mum moved fast or he would have burnt her hand off.

I think she's going to charge you for repainting the wall. There's a big brown patch where he scorched the paint.

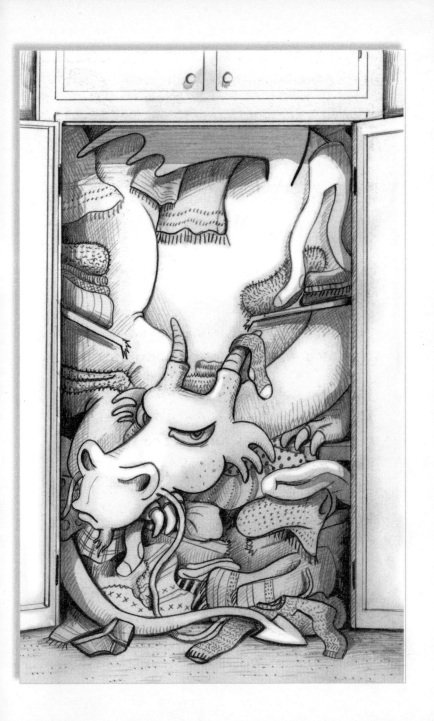

I still think he might be depressed.

We had macaroni cheese for supper. I saved some for Ziggy and left it outside the linen cupboard. When I checked just now, he hadn't even touched it.

But at least he's here and not wandering the streets.

Love from

Eddie

Dear Uncle Morton,

I just wanted to tell you nothing has changed.

Ziggy won't move from the linen cupboard.

He still hasn't eaten a thing. Not even a Malteser.

I'm really quite worried about him.

To be honest, I'm also a bit annoyed, because I had been planning to take him to school today.

When I told Miss Brackenbury why I hadn't brought anything for Show and Tell, she just laughed and said I could do it next week instead.

I hope Ziggy will have come out of the cupboard by then.

Eddie

Hi Eddie,

Sorry I haven't replied before, but we're forbidden from using any electronic devices at the retreat. I have sneaked down to the village to read my mail.

Please tell your mother that I'm very sorry about her linen and will, of course, buy her a new set of everything. And don't worry about Ziggy's appetite: if he gets hungry, he will eat.

Thanks again for looking after him. I would never have been able to come here otherwise.

The retreat is exhausting and strangely wonderful. We are woken at five o'clock in the morning and spend four hours sitting in silence before breakfast. The rest of the day is devoted to yoga, pausing only for a meal of vegetable curry and rice. My mind is clear and my body contorts into shapes that would have been impossible only last week.

Love from your affectionate uncle

Morton

From: Edward Smith-Pickle

To: Morton Pickle

Date: Thursday 20 October

Subject: Important question

Attachments: Egg

Dear Uncle Morton,

Are you sure Ziggy is a boy?

I think he might be a girl.

I mean, I think she might be a girl.

You're probably wondering why I'm thinking this, and the answer is very simple.

She has laid an egg in the linen cupboard.

Now I understand why she likes being in there. Not only is it nice and warm, but she's built herself a nest from Mum's clean sheets and towels.

The egg is green and shiny and about the size of a bike helmet.

Do you think I could take it to school next week for Show and Tell?

I promise I won't drop it.

Ziggy still isn't eating. Mum says she was ravenous when she was pregnant with me and Emily, but maybe dragons are different.

Eddie

Dear Uncle Morton,

There is a tiny crack in the egg. I'm sure it wasn't there yesterday.

Mum says I have to go to school, but I don't want to. What if the baby comes when I'm not here?

She's calling me. I've got to go.

It's so unfair!

If you get this, please, please, please will you ring Mum and tell her someone needs to stay with the egg?

E

Dear Uncle Morton,

I'm glad to say the baby hasn't arrived yet.

When Mum picked us up and brought us home, I went straight upstairs to the linen cupboard.

The egg was still there.

It has changed, though. It's covered in more cracks.

Also it keeps shaking and shuddering as if something is stirring under the surface.

I'm not going to sleep tonight.

Eddie

From: Edward Smith-Pickle

To: Morton Pickle

Date: Saturday 22 October

Subject: It's here

📎 **Attachments:** His first step; Birthday boy

Dear Uncle Morton,

This is the most amazing day of my life. I have just watched a baby dragon being born.

I didn't stay up last night. Mum made me and Emily go to bed.

I tried to sneak out of my room, but she heard me and sent me back.

Then I tried to stay awake in my bed, but I must have drifted off, because when I next opened my eyes, it was 6.43.

I got out of bed and tiptoed down the corridor to the linen cupboard. I thought I would have missed everything, but there was the egg, still in one piece.

It had changed again, though. It was covered in hundreds of little cracks.

I must have stood there for at least half an hour, watching and waiting, but nothing happened.

I was just about to go downstairs and grab some breakfast when the shell cracked open and a leg popped out.

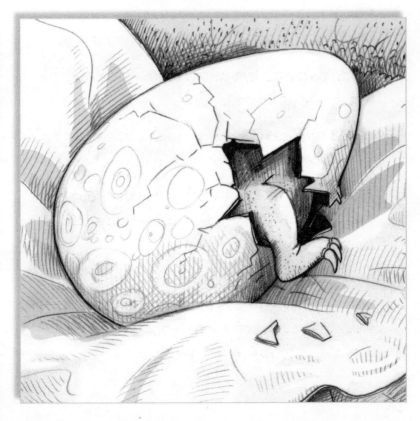

I stayed absolutely still. I don't think I even breathed.

The little green leg wiggled and waggled. I could see the four miniature claws stretching and flexing as if they were trying to find something to hold on to.

I thought Ziggy might get involved, but she just sat there, watching.

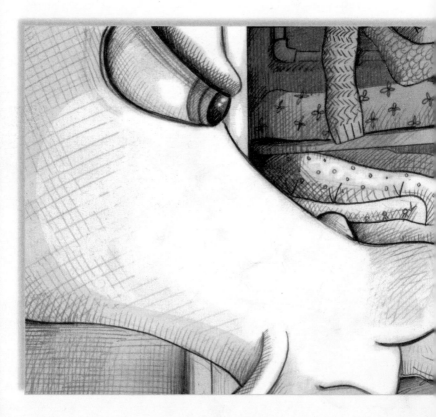

Suddenly more shell shattered and another leg popped out.

Then a bit of a body. And a head.

There it was.

A baby dragon about the size of a small pigeon.

It pulled itself out of the egg and rolled onto the pillowcase, leaving a trail of broken shell.

If I had picked it up (which I didn't) it would have fitted in the palm of my hand.

That was when Ziggy finally seemed to notice her baby. She leaned over and started licking it.

I ran downstairs and grabbed some food from the fridge. Ziggy is still refusing to eat, but the baby seems to be hungry. So far it's drunk a bowl of milk and eaten two cold potatoes and half a sausage.

I wanted to give it some chocolate as a treat, but I don't know if sweets are good for babies.

I wish you were here to see it.

Love from

Eddie

Hi Eddie,

I was overjoyed to get your email and the beautiful pictures. What wonderful news! I'm delighted, and not a little envious. One of my greatest ambitions has always been to witness the birth of a dragon.

I also feel very stupid. It had never occurred to me that Ziggy might be female. I could have checked, I suppose, but I know a man who lost three fingers doing that, so I'd never tried.

Which reminds me: don't touch the baby!
It might bite.

I have discussed my circumstances with
Swami Ticklemore and he recommended
that I did not stop the retreat early. Would
you mind taking care of Ziggy and her child
for a few more days? I should be able to
leave, as planned, at the end of the week.

Morton

From: Edward Smith–Pickle

To: Morton Pickle

Date: Sunday 23 October

Subject: Arthur

Attachments: Happy baby

Dear Uncle Morton,

You don't have to worry about the baby biting. He's very friendly and sweet. All he does is play and eat and sleep.

He poos too, but they're very small, so I don't mind clearing them up.

Emily says he's the cutest thing she's ever seen.

I have called him Arthur. I hope you like the name. If you would prefer something else, please let me know ASAP.

Obviously I don't actually know if he's a boy or a girl, and I'm not going to try and find out, but he looks very boyish to me.

If he ever lays an egg, could you change his name to Gwendoline? That was Emily's choice, and I promised she could have it if he turned out to be a she.

Right now he is snuggling up with Ziggy in the linen cupboard. Mum is cooking a big spaghetti bolognese for all of us to have for supper, dragons included.

Love from

Eddie

From: Edward Smith-Pickle

To: Morton Pickle

Date: Monday 24 October

Subject: Help!

Attachments: Him; Mum fights back

Dear Uncle Morton,

You've got to help us. There's a massive dragon in our garden and he won't go away.

He arrived just before bedtime. Mum was running the bath when we heard a terrible bang.

Mum thought the roof had collapsed. I was worried an asteroid had crashed into the house.

We ran outside to have a look.

The first thing we saw was the TV aerial lying in the middle of the garden.

About twenty tiles from the roof had fallen down there too.

Then we saw why.

An enormous dragon was sitting on our house. Smoke was trickling out of his nostrils, and his tail was flicking from side to side, knocking more tiles off the roof.

Ziggy must have heard the noise too, because she came outside to see what was going on.

As soon as she saw the dragon, she breathed a huge burst of flames in his direction. I thought it was her way of saying hello, but I soon realised she was telling him to get lost.

It didn't work. The big dragon flew down and charged towards her, gushing flames from his nostrils as if he was planning to roast her alive.

Ziggy sprinted back into the house, pushing Arthur in front of her.

The big dragon actually tried to follow us inside, but Mum chased him out again.

She bashed him on the nose with a broom.

I said she should be careful, but Mum said she wasn't scared of some silly dragon, however fierce he might look.

She just rang you seven times. I said you weren't listening to your messages, but she kept leaving them anyway.

If you get this, please call us ASAP.

Eddie

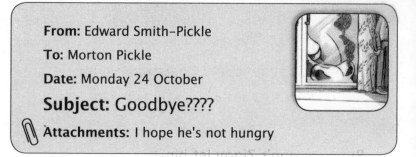

Dear Uncle Morton,

The big dragon is still here. He's lying on the patio, watching us through the windows, as if he's waiting for the perfect moment to smash through the glass and come inside.

He has scary eyes.

Do you think he could be Arthur's dad?
Is that why he's here? Has he come to see
his son?

But why won't Ziggy let him?

Can dragons get divorced?

Mum says I have to go to bed now.

If you don't get any more messages from
me, it's because I've been eaten by a
massive dragon.

Eddie

From: Edward Smith–Pickle

To: Morton Pickle

Date: Tuesday 25 October

Subject: I'm still here

Attachments: Yummy Mummies

Dear Uncle Morton,

We're all still here. Including the dragon. He spent the night in the garden. There's not much left of Mum's plants.

I think he's been trying to talk to Ziggy. He's certainly been breathing a lot of fire in her direction and making some strange barking noises.

She must be able to hear him, but she pretends not to. She's just been lying in the kitchen with her head in Mum's lap.

I don't know why they're suddenly such good friends.

When I asked Mum, she said "Female solidarity".

I've got to go to school now. I'm taking Arthur for Show and Tell. He's coming with me in a shoebox. I hope Miss Brackenbury likes him.

Love from

Eddie

From: Edward Smith-Pickle
To: Morton Pickle
Date: Tuesday 25 October
Subject: Stuck
Attachments: No exit

Dear Uncle Morton,

It's me again.

We couldn't leave the house. The big dragon blocked our way.

Mum told him to step aside, but he took no notice.

They stared at one another for a long time.

You know how fierce Mum can be, but the dragon didn't even blink.

One of them had to move first and it turned out to be the dragon.

He breathed a sizzling jet of flame in our direction.

Mum shoved me and Emily back inside,
then slammed the front door.

We tried to sneak out twice more, but he
was always waiting for us.

So we can't go to school, which is cool.

Maybe this big dragon isn't so bad,
after all.

Eddie

Dear Uncle Morton,

I was wrong. Staying at home is even worse than going to school. Mum made us do sums all morning. She's going to make us do more this afternoon.

Luckily I've got an idea for how to get out of here.

I remembered what you said about once taming a massive dragon in Outer Mongolia with a rucksack full of chocolate.

I'm going to try the same trick with this one.

Wish me luck!

Eddie

Dear Uncle Morton,

It didn't work.

Mum saw me heading for the front door with an armful of sweets and confiscated the lot.

Now she and Ziggy are sitting on the sofa, watching telly and sharing a box of Maltesers.

I told Mum she was eating our only chance of escape, but she just laughed.

I think we're going to be stuck in here for ever.

Eddie

Dear Uncle Morton,

I know you're not supposed to talk till Friday, but *please* could you call us?

Today is even worse than yesterday.

The dragons have been fighting all morning. The big one broke down the back door and rampaged through the house. He knocked over the telly and broke our kitchen table in half. Also he's knocked almost all the pictures off the wall.

We had to lock ourselves in the loo.

We finally came out when the house was quiet.

Ziggy had chased the big dragon into the garden. I don't know how she did it.

40

She and Arthur are lying on what's left of the sofa. Every single cushion has been burst open. There are feathers everywhere.

Emily is very upset because we've got nowhere to sit.

I'm more worried about what the big dragon will do next.

Mum just rang the retreat and spoke to Swami Ticklemore. He said you couldn't be disturbed.

Mum said it was an emergency, but Swami Ticklemore wouldn't change his mind.

If you get this, please call Mum ASAP.

Eddie

From: Morton Pickle
To: Edward Smith-Pickle
Date: Wednesday 26 October
Subject: Re: Please call us!

Attachments: Meditation

Hi Eddie,

I'm very sorry, but I can't leave the retreat early. Swami Ticklemore says I would do permanent damage to my inner peace.

I shall hurry out of here at dawn on Friday and come straight to your house.

I don't know exactly why the big dragon is bothering you, but I should imagine he is no different to any other proud father and simply wants to meet his son. Maybe you should let them spend some time together?

If that's not possible, why don't the three of you go and stay in a hotel?

You can tell your mother that I will, of course, pay for the room.

M

Dear Uncle Morton,

Mum didn't like your idea about staying in a hotel.

She looked at me as if I was a complete idiot. Then she spent about fifteen minutes saying why oh why was she surrounded by such stupid, selfish men.

I think she means you, Dad and the dragon.

She might have meant me too. I'm not sure.

Anyway, Uncle Morton, couldn't you talk to Swami Ticklemore again and ask for special permission to leave early?

Otherwise you might have to pay for more than a night in a hotel.

If the dragons carry on like this, you'll have to buy us a new house.

Eddie

Dear Uncle Morton,

You won't believe what just happened.

I was in the sitting room with Arthur and Ziggy when the big dragon appeared at the window. He started breathing fire and making those strange barky noises.

Obviously I don't know what he was saying, but I could see Ziggy listening to him. Then she seemed to be talking to him. Finally she went to the door.

She looked at me. I knew what she wanted. I undid the latch. The three of us walked outside – Ziggy first, then Arthur, and finally me.

The big dragon started flapping his wings, slowly at first, then faster and faster.

Arthur hopped onto his back.

They lifted into the air.

I thought this was the last time I would see them. I wished Mum and Emily had been there to say goodbye. Then I turned to look at Ziggy and saw she was lowering her neck down to the ground.

There was a strange expression in her eyes.

I realised it was an invitation.

I'm so glad Mum and Emily were upstairs, because if they'd been watching, they would have screamed at me to come back inside.

But I was alone. So I could do what I wanted.

I lifted my leg over Ziggy's neck and clambered onto her back. As soon as I was settled, her wings flapped and we went up – past the trees – and up – above the roofs – and up, and up and up and up and up and up.

I was flying!

I knew I shouldn't look down, but I couldn't stop myself. The garden was already tiny.

I could see the other dragon above us, his huge body silhouetted against the sky.

Higher and higher we went. Till we were
swallowed by the clouds. I couldn't see
anything except whiteness. It was really
chilly too. If Ziggy hadn't been so warm,
I would have been frozen solid.

Suddenly we broke through the top of the clouds and we were in sunshine. The big dragon was just ahead of us. With a few flaps of her wings, Ziggy was alongside him.

I could see Arthur hopping around on his dad's back, but I held on as tightly as I could, wrapping my arms around Ziggy's neck. I didn't have wings to save me if I slipped off.

Suddenly the big dragon flipped over. Then up again.

Ziggy did it too.

For a moment I was upside down!

Next they both looped the loop.

Three times.

It was like being in the Red Arrows.

Up and down we went. Round and round. The two dragons taking turns to do tricks as if they were saying to each other, *Look at me! Can you do this too?*

I thought I might be sick, but actually it was Arthur who was.

I suppose he is only four days old.

The others must have thought he'd had enough then, because suddenly we were diving down again, heading for the ground.

We were going so fast, I thought we'd crash through the house. But at the last moment, the two dragons pulled back and we landed gently on the patio.

The three of them are dozing now, but I wanted to come inside and tell you all about it.

Eddie

From: Edward Smith-Pickle

To: Morton Pickle

Date: Wednesday 26 October

Subject: He's gone

Attachments: Quiet time

Dear Uncle Morton,

Don't worry about leaving the retreat early. You can stay as long as you like. That big dragon has gone and I don't think he's coming back.

Mum says he probably has another girlfriend somewhere, and maybe he does, but I'm sure that's not really why he's left.

I think he came here to see his son, and now he has, so he can go.

Taking Arthur into the air must have been his way of saying goodbye.

I suppose it's the same as Dad taking me to the cinema before he drives back to Cardiff.

Everything is very peaceful here now it's just the five of us.

Mum and Ziggy are watching a black and white movie on telly.

Arthur and Emily are playing Monopoly. Neither of them know the rules. They're just pushing the pieces around the board and making a mess of the money. Emily keeps giggling and Arthur is blowing little spurts of smoke through his nostrils.

I hope you enjoy your last day at the retreat, and see you on Friday.

Eddie

From: Morton Pickle
To: Edward Smith-Pickle
Date: Saturday 29 October
Subject: Re: He's gone
Attachments: Home sweet home; Clipping

Hi Eddie,

We are finally home after an interminable train journey and a stormy ride in Mr McDougall's boat. The house feels much smaller with two dragons, even if one of them is only a baby. When Arthur grows up, I'll have to build him and Ziggy a home of their own.

I want to thank you again for looking after them so well.

Please tell your mother that I really am very sorry about all the trouble that they caused.

You probably won't like me saying so, but I do think she was right about Arthur. Having a pet is a serious responsibility.

If I were you, I would accept her offer.
I know gerbils aren't exactly exciting, but
you can always get something bigger
when you're older.

Will you please also tell your mother that I was entirely serious about the retreat. I could see how stressed she is. Nothing would make her feel better than a week of silence and yoga.

While she is with Swami Ticklemore, you and Emily could stay with me. I know Ziggy and Arthur would love to see you – as would I.

Lots of love from your affectionate uncle

Morton

PS Did you see this?

Saturday 29th October

The Scotsman

IS IT A BIRD?
IS IT A PLANE?
NO, IT'S A DRAGON!

Photograph courtesy of Annabel Birkinstock

Passengers on a British Airways flight to Paris were treated to an extraordinary spectacle when two enormous green creatures flew past their plane.

Neither the pilot nor air traffic controllers noticed anything unusual, but at least a hundred passengers are convinced that they were visited by dragons.

Fashion consultant Annabel Birkinstock could hardly believe her eyes. She flies from London to Paris at

Fashion consultant Annabel Birkinstock

least once a month, and has seen everything from David Beckham to the Eiffel Tower, but she was astonished when she looked out of the window and spotted a dragon flying past.

"At first I thought it might be a huge bird," said the shocked twenty-seven-year-old. "But I've never heard of birds breathing smoke from their nostrils."

Aviation expert Graham Tulse has examined photographs taken by passengers on the plane and said the "dragons" were probably just an illusion caused by sunlight and cloud cover.

"The stewards must have been serving too many free drinks," he scoffed. "One of the passengers even claimed there was a boy riding on a dragon's back!"

Annabel Birkinstock doesn't agree. "I know what I saw," she told us last night. "Those weren't rainbows or shadows. They were undoubtedly dragons."

If you have enjoyed
The Dragonsitter Takes Off,
you might also enjoy these other
books by Josh Lacey. . .

The Dragonsitter

Josh Lacey

Illustrated by Garry Parsons

A hilarious novel for younger readers by the author of the Grk books.

'Dear Uncle Morton. You'd better get on a plane right now and come back here. Your dragon has eaten Jemima. Emily loved that rabbit.'

It had sounded so easy: Edward was going to look after Uncle Morton's unusual pet for a week while he went on holiday. But soon the fridge is empty, the curtains are blazing, and the postman is fleeing down the garden path.

'A witty book that deserves to be read and reread.'
Books for Keeps

9781849394192 £4.99

THE grk BOOKS

When Timothy Malt finds a small white dog sitting outside his house and decides to adopt him, he little suspects what adventures he is signing up for. He flies a helicopter in Eastern Europe, exposes an international art thief in New York, and chases bank robbers through the jungles of Brazil!

WHIZZ ROUND THE WORLD WITH A GRK BOOK!

9781842703847

9781842705278

9781842705537

9781842705599

9781842706602

9781842706619

9781842709313

9781842709320

Instructions for dragonsitting

As you know, Ziggy has an excellent
appetite and will happily snack all day long,
but I try to restrict his mealtimes to the
same as mine.

He will eat anything except curry and
porridge.

Please don't give him ice cream. It plays
havoc with his digestion. He does love it,
though, so don't leave any within reach.

Don't forget: dragons will do anything for
chocolate! I usually keep several bars of
Cadbury's Fruit and Nut for emergencies.

Ziggy isn't an energetic creature. He usually
sleeps all night and most of the day, and
requires only a little gentle exercise. If he's
feeling restless, he'll take himself for a quick
flight and be home in time for tea.

I usually let him outside to do his business
after breakfast and before bedtime.
Accidents will happen and I shall, of course,
recompense you for any damage.

He is perfectly happy curling up anywhere, even the hardest cold stone floor, but will be grateful for a couple of cushions. Please don't let him sleep in your bed - I don't want him getting into bad habits.

I have clipped his claws, so you shouldn't need to. If you do, I recommend garden shears.

If his rash recurs, call Isobel Macintyre, our vet in Lower Biskett. See other sheet for number. She knows Ziggy well and could help in a crisis.

If you have a non-medical emergency, try Mr McDougall. I'll leave you the number for the ashram, but it will probably go unanswered. As the swami says, "Silence is the sound of inner peace."

Thanks again for looking after Ziggy and see you on Friday.

M

From: Morton Pickle

To: Alice Brackenbury

Date: Tuesday 8 November

Subject: Re: School visit

Dear Miss Brackenbury,

Thank you so much for your delightful email. There was no need to introduce yourself; Eddie has told me how much he enjoys your lessons, which, I can assure you, is a great compliment from my nephew.

I'm touched and flattered by your suggestion that I should visit the school and give a talk about my travels. I have indeed been to some extraordinary places, and I always enjoy chatting about the months that I spent tagging penguins in Patagonia or my voyage in a leaky canoe down the furthest tributaries of the Amazon.

However, I chose some years ago to come and live on a small island, just off the coast of Scotland, and I have many duties here. I am also, I must confess, a nervous public speaker, and your students would probably be bored by my ramblings.

Instead of myself, may I offer a copy of my book? It will be published by a small press later this year – the title is: The Winged Serpents of Zavkhan: In Search of the Dragons of Outer Mongolia.

I shall send a couple of copies to Eddie and ask him to bring one to school. You might like to read a few pages to your class. Obviously I wouldn't want to encourage schoolchildren to hunt for dragons – they are quiet creatures and prefer to be left alone – but I should like to inspire the younger generation with a respect for wildlife and a longing for adventure.

With all best wishes

Morton